Sea Monsters Don't Ride Motorcycles

There are more books about the Bailey School Kids!
Have you read these adventures?

Sea Monsters Don't Ride Motorcycles

by Debbie Dadey
and
Marcia Thornton Jones

illustrated by John Steven Gurney

A
LITTLE APPLE
PAPERBACK

SCHOLASTIC INC.
New York   Toronto   London   Auckland   Sydney
Mexico City   New Delhi   Hong Kong

To Barbara Beckham and
Randy Thornton — MTJ

To the people at
Scholastic who gave us our start.
Many thanks! — DD

ISBN 0-439-04401-4

12 11 10 9 8 7 6   3 4 5/0

Printed in the U.S.A.   40

First Scholastic printing, March 2000

Contents

1

Sheldon City Raceway

Zoom! Zoom!

"What is taking my grandmother so long?" Eddie shouted above the roar of motorcycles. "It will be Christmas before she gets here."

Eddie and his friends Melody, Howie, and Liza stood at the entrance to the Sheldon City Raceway. A bright red sign hung over their heads and a ticket booth stood to the right. Ten people waited in line to buy tickets. Inside the entrance the stands were almost full. A few motorcycles were rolling up to the track and racing their engines, even though the races didn't start for another five minutes.

"I'm going to explode if she makes us miss any of the action," Eddie complained, straining his neck to see the motorcycles.

The crowd was in his way and all he saw was the flash of a chrome bumper.

Liza put her hands on her hips and stared at Eddie. "Don't be so mean. Your grandmother is older. It takes her longer to walk. We should have waited for her instead of running ahead."

"That's right," Melody agreed. "After all, your grandmother was nice enough to bring us all the way to Sheldon City for the weekend."

"She's going to take us to the beach and everything," Howie added. "Instead of complaining, you should help her out."

Eddie grinned. The crowd had moved through the gate and he could see inside. He pulled his blue baseball cap off his red hair and pointed toward a line of motorcycles parked just inside the entrance. "I know how I could help my grandmother. I could get her one of those motorcycles."

Liza giggled. "That doesn't look like something a grandmother would drive."

2

"Wow!" Howie said. "I wish my dad would get *that* one." Howie pointed to a slime-green motorcycle that stood dead center in a group of black motorcycles. The shiny green motorcycle had bright electric-yellow stripes running down the side and a skull painted on the gas tank.

"I want that one!" Eddie said. "It's the coolest motorcycle ever."

"What's that writing on the side?" Liza asked, squinting to read it in the bright sunlight.

"It's probably the owner's name," Melody suggested.

Eddie shook his head. "No, it's the name of the motorcycle."

"How do you know?" Liza asked.

What Eddie said next gave Howie goose bumps, even though it was a warm day.

"My eyesight is perfect," Eddie bragged. "The name of that motorcycle is easy to read. It's called The Monster."

2

The Monster

"Let's take a closer look at The Monster," Eddie suggested as his grandmother finished paying for the tickets.

Liza shook her head. "No, the races are starting. We need to find a seat." The four kids and Eddie's grandmother headed toward the grandstands.

"I hope there's shade," Howie said. "It's really hot today."

"I'm so hot I could jump into the ocean with my clothes on," Melody said, wiping sweat off her forehead.

Eddie's grandmother nodded. "That might not be such a bad idea," she said. "We'll do a little wading to cool off after the races."

Liza smiled at Eddie's grandmother. "You are very nice."

"Thank you, Liza," Eddie's grand-mother said. "It's always good to hear that. Why don't you take a seat while I get drinks?"

The kids sat on the bleachers and watched as more racers hopped onto their motorcycles. "Look," Liza said, pointing to The Monster motorcycle. "Someone is getting on Eddie's favorite motorcycle."

"And the rider is dripping wet," Melody said. She was right. The rider was dressed in black leather like all the other racers, but The Monster's rider looked like he had just crawled out of the nearby ocean. Water puddled around two big black boots.

All the racers positioned themselves at the starting line and waited. Their engines roared in the afternoon air.

"It's so noisy I can't hear myself think!" Liza shouted, putting her hands over her ears.

"Who needs to think?" Eddie yelled.

"Just watch." The gun fired, the flag was lowered, and the racers blasted off. They roared around the track.

"Go, Monster!" Eddie shrieked. One small black motorcycle didn't make the first turn and skidded to a halt near a wooden fence.

Liza gasped. "This is dangerous."

Eddie's grandmother returned and handed the kids their drinks, but Eddie was much too excited to drink. Four racers pulled away from the pack. The green Monster motorcycle was one of them.

"The Monster is going to win!" Melody clapped.

Howie shook his head. "They still have to go another lap."

"I don't like this," Liza muttered. She closed her eyes as another motorcycle fell over and a rider tumbled to safety.

The motorcycles sped around the track. The Monster was neck and neck with a big black motorcycle with a red stripe.

"Come on!" Eddie shouted and jumped up from his seat. When he did, his drink flew in the air. Soda splashed all over Howie. But Eddie didn't even notice. "You can do it, Monster!" he yelled.

The Monster edged ahead of the black motorcycle and won the race. "All right!" Melody and Eddie cheered.

Liza opened her eyes. "Whew! I'm glad that's over." Then she looked at Howie and giggled. Eddie's spilled drink dripped from Howie's nose and ears.

Melody laughed, too. "You look like something that just crawled up from the depths of the sea."

Howie didn't say anything. Instead, he stared at the winning racer. The crowd cheered even louder as the racer took off the black leather jacket and helmet.

Eddie didn't cheer. His face turned gray. "Hey," Eddie shouted. "That's no guy!"

3

Tough with a Capital T

"Cool," Melody said with a smile. "A woman beat all those guys. That just proves that girls can do anything boys do—only better!"

Eddie curled his fingers into a fist and held it right under Melody's nose. "The only thing this proves is that girls like you should watch what they say!"

Liza grabbed Eddie's fist and pulled it back. "Melody's right," she told Eddie. "Girls can do whatever boys do. But," she added and nodded toward the winning racer, "I've never seen a woman like that before."

The kids stared at the winner as she propped her helmet on the back of The Monster motorcycle and slipped out of her leather jacket. The woman had long

10

wavy greenish hair and a tattoo on her arm that looked like a giant sea serpent. She laughed and poured a glass of water over her head to cool off just as a group of fans and a reporter from WMTJ surrounded her. The water rushed through her green hair and dripped off her chin, looking exactly like sea foam.

"Most women have poofy hair and wear lipstick," Howie said, "like my mom."

"A mom who looked like The Monster's rider would be cool," Eddie said. "I bet she'd let her kids zoom around town on her motorcycle."

"Don't be too sure," Howie said. "Any woman riding a motorcycle called The Monster might be tough on kids."

Liza nodded. "And that woman fits the definition of tough with a capital T."

"Not as tough as her motorcycle," Eddie said and jumped down off the bleachers. "I want to have a closer look!"

Eddie didn't wait for anybody. He

rushed off the bleachers and joined the crowd surrounding the winner. His friends helped Eddie's grandmother off the bleachers before following.

They all crowded close as the reporter finished interviewing the winner. "This has been an exclusive interview with Jessie MacFarland," the reporter said and smiled into the camera. Eddie jumped behind the reporter and made a face just as the camera lights went out.

Jessie MacFarland watched as Howie, Melody, and Liza looked at her bike. The Monster was one snazzy motorcycle. When Eddie asked if he could sit on it, Jessie nodded.

"Wow!" Eddie said and hopped on.

Liza giggled. "I don't know which is scarier. Eddie or The Monster!" While the kids took turns on the motorcycle, Jessie MacFarland took a pouch of food from a nearby cooler.

Howie gulped. "That looks just like seaweed," he whispered to Melody. Even

13

though he was whispering, Jessie Mac-Farland must have heard every word. She smiled at Howie and held out the pouch. "Would you like to try a pinch of my snack?" she offered.

Melody shook her head and Howie said, "No thanks." Liza's face turned a sickly color and she shook her head. But Eddie grabbed the pouch and stuck his nose inside for a big whiff.

"Phe-eewww!" Eddie gasped and held the pouch as far away from him as he could. "This smells like something that died on the beach."

Eddie's grandmother snatched the pouch away from Eddie and gave him a warning look. Then she smiled at Jessie. "I think trying new things is exciting. I would love some of your snack."

"No, Grandma," Eddie warned. "What if it's slimy and tastes like boogers?"

Eddie's grandmother frowned. "Non-sense," she said. "Trying new food adds

spice to life. And if you don't watch your mouth I might make you eat spinach and brussels sprouts for dinner!"

Eddie's face turned a color that matched Jessie's snack and he didn't say another word as his grandmother took a bite. She closed her eyes and chewed. Finally she swallowed. When she did, she looked at Jessie and smiled. "How delightful! What did I just eat?"

Jessie smiled. "Kelp is one of my favorite treats," she told Eddie's grandmother. "You may have the rest because I have another snack right here in this cooler."

Eddie stared in horror as his grandmother swallowed more kelp. Things got even worse when she closed the package and looked straight at Eddie. "This is so wonderful, I think I'll save the rest for our dinner."

Eddie groaned and held his stomach as if he'd just caught a terrible flu bug. His friends didn't notice. They were too busy staring at Jessie as she dug in the cooler and took out a tiny silver fish.

Then, right before their eyes, Jessie MacFarland swallowed the fish whole.

4

Just Like a Fish

The sun warmed up the bleachers, and by the end of the races the kids were really hot. "Let's hit the beach," Eddie said.

His grandmother nodded. "After all," she said, "why come to Sheldon's seashore if you're not planning on building a sand castle?"

As soon as his grandmother stopped the van at the beach, the kids jumped out and raced over the hot sand. They had to stop and wait for Eddie's grandmother to climb the sand dune before getting in the water.

"It always takes her too long to get anywhere," Eddie complained.

"Maybe she's not slow," Liza pointed out. "Maybe we're just fast."

"Liza's right," Melody said. "We run everywhere. That's why we always beat your grandmother."

Eddie shook his head and pointed to the top of the sand dune. "But we don't stop and count windows."

Howie, Liza, and Melody looked where Eddie pointed. Sure enough, Eddie's grandmother had stopped and was staring at a nearby building as if she were counting every window. Finally she turned and headed toward the kids.

"Isn't that a nice building?" she asked Eddie. "Wouldn't you like to live in a beach resort like that?"

Eddie looked at his grandmother as if she had just sprouted fish scales and fins. "I don't want to daydream," he said. "I want to play!" And then he turned and jumped into the waves.

Eddie splashed his friends as soon as they joined him. Then they all dived into the waves and let the water tumble them back onto the sand.

The waves on the shore made a constant roar. That's probably why the kids didn't notice anything else at first. When they finally did, it was almost too late.

The Monster thundered over the sand dune and onto the beach. Sand scattered under its wheels as it headed straight for the kids.

"We're going to be squashed by The Monster," Liza squealed.

Jessie MacFarland stopped The Monster just in time. She jumped to the ground and pulled off her helmet. "A swim is the perfect way to end a great day," she told the kids. Then she peeled off her leather jumpsuit. Howie noticed that Jessie had on a green bathing suit that looked like it was covered with tiny scales. It blended right in with the sea serpent tattoo on her arm.

Jessie ran into the surf so fast she became a blur. As soon as the water reached her knees, Jessie disappeared beneath a wave that was rolling toward shore.

"Where did she go?" Eddie asked.

"Did she get washed out to sea?" Liza asked.

"There she is!" Melody yelled and pointed out into the ocean.

Jessie was already so far out her head was just a tiny dot. "It's not safe to swim that far from shore," Howie said. "She better come back."

The words were barely out when Jessie turned and started swimming back toward them.

"Wow," Eddie said with a whistle. "I've never seen anybody swim that fast."

Liza nodded. "She's swimming just like a fish."

As soon as Liza said that, Howie started to cough and sputter. Melody pounded on his back and Eddie grabbed Howie around the chest. Howie pushed his friends away. "I'm not choking," he told them. "I was just thinking about what Liza said."

"I never think about what Liza says," Eddie said.

Liza glared at Eddie, but Howie ignored them both. "We *have* met somebody as fast as Jessie," he told his friends.

"Who are you talking about?" Eddie asked.

Howie couldn't answer because Jessie was crawling out of the ocean. Water dripped from her fingers and nose. One piece of seaweed was stuck between her toes and another piece dangled from her green hair.

"You are the fastest swimmer in the world," Liza told Jessie.

"You're as fast in the water as you are on your motorcycle," Eddie added.

Howie wasn't smiling when he nodded. "You remind me of somebody else," he said. "She was fast, too."

Jessie looked Howie in the eyes. "Who might that be?" she asked.

"We had a running coach," Howie told her. "And she had a name that sounded just like yours."

"That's right," Liza squealed. "Nessie MacFarland was a very good coach — if it hadn't been for her we wouldn't have won our race against the Sheldon City Sharks!"

"So," Jessie said. "My cousin has been here! I knew it was only a matter of time before I hunted her down!"

5

Tattoo

"Indoor pool!" Eddie shouted. "Let's go right away."

Eddie's grandmother smiled. "First we have to check into the Seaside Resort Hotel. I'll be done in a jiffy." Eddie's grandmother hurried off to the hotel desk, leaving the four kids sitting in the lobby.

"It's so nice of your grandmother to bring us here for the weekend," Liza told Eddie.

Melody nodded. "Don't you think so, Howie?"

Howie stared out the hotel window toward the ocean, as if he were in a different world.

"Earth to Howie," Eddie beeped and

nudged Howie on the arm. "Earth to Howie."

Howie looked at his friends. "I'm worried," he admitted.

"About what?" Liza asked. "This is a perfect weekend."

"We don't even have homework," Eddie said with a smile.

"But we do have a problem," Howie told his friends. "Her name is Jessie Mac-Farland."

Liza shook her head. "Jessie is nice," she said. "After all, she let us sit on her motorcycle. An ordinary person probably wouldn't have done that."

"You're on the right track," Howie agreed. "Jessie is no ordinary person. Didn't you notice that tattoo?"

"It was cool," Eddie said, leaning back into the green sofa.

"Yes," Howie said. "But it was a sea monster tattoo."

"I don't care if it was a Peter Pan tattoo," Eddie snapped. "Jessie has the coolest bike ever."

"Don't you get it?" Howie asked.

Liza, Melody, and Eddie looked at Howie and shrugged. "What's to get?" Melody asked.

"Do you remember Nessie MacFarland?" Howie asked.

Melody nodded. "Sure, she was the coach who helped us win the race against Sheldon City."

"Don't you remember thinking that Nessie MacFarland was the Loch Ness Monster?"

Liza squealed. "That's right! I was so scared of her."

Eddie propped his feet up on the glass coffee table. "That was silly. Nessie was probably just an ordinary coach."

"I don't think so," Howie admitted. "And if Nessie was the Loch Ness Monster and Jessie is her cousin, can't you figure out what that makes Jessie?"

6

When Monsters Collide

"You mean we were swimming with a sea monster?" Liza cried.

Melody giggled. "What's wrong with that? We go to school every day with a monster named Eddie."

Eddie jumped up from the sofa. "I'm not a monster!" he shouted.

Howie hopped up and patted Eddie's shoulder. "Let's just stay calm and try to figure out what a sea monster is doing near Bailey City."

"That's easy," Liza said. "Jessie told us she was looking for her cousin."

Howie ran his hand through his hair and gulped. "What would happen if a sea monster and the Loch Ness Monster clashed right here on Sheldon Beach?"

Eddie sat back down on the sofa and

laughed. "That would be great. Maybe we could get front row tickets."

Melody laughed, too. "I could borrow my dad's video camera and we could make a movie out of it."

"We'd become famous movie producers," Liza said with a giggle. "We could name our first movie *When Monsters Collide.*"

Howie rolled his eyes. "Will you stop fooling around? I'm serious."

"This is no place to be serious," Eddie told his friend. "We're at the beach. We're supposed to have a good time."

"That's right," Melody agreed.

"After all," Liza added, "sea monsters don't ride motorcycles."

Howie stood up and put his hands on his hips. "I guess there's only one way to find out what's going on. We have to spy on Jessie at the racetrack."

"Well," Eddie admitted, "I do love to spy."

"Do you think your grandmother will take us back to the track?" Howie asked.

Eddie nodded. "I think my grandmother liked the races better than we did. I'm sure she'd want to go back."

"Okay," Howie said. "Then it's agreed. We go back to the racetrack and see if we can snoop out a monster."

Just then Eddie's grandmother appeared. "Let's go for that swim in the pool," she said.

"All right!" Eddie shouted as if he'd forgotten everything Howie had said. He raced after his grandmother. Liza and Melody followed Eddie, leaving Howie behind.

"What about the sea monster?" Howie asked, but no one heard him.

7

Waterlogged

Eddie splashed. He kicked. Then he splashed some more. He dived under the water and pretended to be a sea monster in the depths of the Bermuda Triangle. He sneaked up behind Liza and Melody to grab their ankles. He surfaced like a giant alligator and squirted water all over Howie. Then he kicked his feet like a giant walrus and sent a wall of water at his grandmother. It was only a matter of minutes before they were all thoroughly soaked.

Liza squealed. Eddie's grandmother laughed. "You're worse than any monster living in the ocean," Melody said with a giggle.

But Howie wasn't laughing. He waited until Eddie's grandmother swam to the

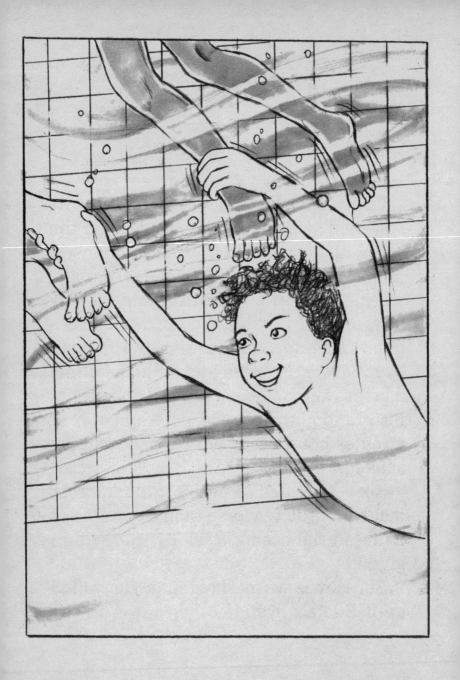

deep end of the pool before pulling his friends close. "We have to solve this sea monster mystery," he told them. "Before it's too late."

"I think your head is waterlogged," Eddie told him. "There are no such things as sea monsters."

"Then you won't be afraid to go back to the track with me," Howie said.

"The only thing I'm afraid of is your imagination," Eddie told his friend.

As soon as they dried off, the kids pulled Eddie's grandmother toward the van. She didn't argue when she found out they wanted to go back to the race-track.

"Those motorcycles are beautiful," she said as she parked the van at the track. "I wonder what it would feel like to race one."

"Like this," Eddie yelled as he jumped out of the van. He pretended he was riding a motorcycle and varoomed around the van until everyone had climbed out and was ready to head to the bleachers.

But Eddie's grandmother didn't go to the bleachers. She headed straight for Jessie. Howie, Melody, Liza, and Eddie had to hurry to catch up. Eddie's grandmother stopped when she reached Jessie and The Monster. Jessie was busy talking with the track manager.

"For once, my cousin was right," Jessie was saying. "This is a very nice area. If this racing season goes well I might just stay and build one of those beach resorts with all my winnings."

"Oh no," Howie mumbled. "This is even worse than I thought. A beach resort is the perfect place for a sea monster to live. She'll be close to the sea where she could swim with the rest of her sea monster relatives. All they'll have to do is grab a couple of kids to nibble on when they get hungry."

"Shhh," Melody warned. "She might hear you."

"Besides," Liza whispered, "wanting to live near the beach doesn't make Jessie a sea monster."

But what they overhead next made them all turn pale. Eddie's grandmother smiled. "Living at a beach resort is a wonderful idea," she said.

"Are you really thinking about moving to the beach?" Jessie asked.

Eddie's grandmother smiled. "I'm always interested in trying new things. Maybe moving to a resort would be an exciting new adventure!"

Howie turned to his friends. His face was as pale as sand. "If Eddie's grandmother moves to the beach," he said, "that would only mean one thing... Eddie would have to move, too!"

"I don't want to move," Eddie moaned. "I've lived in Bailey City since first grade."

"Howie's right," Liza said. "We have to do something before Eddie ends up living in a sea monsters' paradise!"

8

Sea Monsters' Paradise

Howie pulled his friends away from Eddie's grandmother and Jessie. They were so busy talking about the beach resort they probably wouldn't have heard the kids whispering, but Howie didn't want to take the chance.

"There's only one thing to do," Howie told his friends. "We have to keep Jessie from racing."

"We can't keep The Monster off the track," Eddie argued. "It's the best motorcycle here."

"I don't like that idea, either," Liza said softly. "It doesn't seem fair to keep Jessie from her dream of being a motorcycle champion."

"Jessie is earning more money with every race she wins," Howie explained. "I believe she plans to open a beach resort with that money, right here at Sheldon Beach. It sounds like she already has Eddie's grandmother ready to move in!"

"There has to be another way," Melody added.

"We could just tell Eddie's grand-mother that Jessie is a monster," Liza suggested.

Eddie looked in Liza's eyes. "Do you honestly believe my grandmother would believe that?" he asked.

Liza sighed and shook her head.

"Why don't you tell your grandmother that you don't want to move?" Melody asked.

"Because she'll say the same thing she says when I tell her I don't want to eat creamed pea casserole," he told her.

"What's that?" Howie asked.

"She tells me to stop complaining and try it anyway," Eddie said just like his grandmother would say it.

Melody nodded. "Grown-ups always say things like that," she admitted.

"We have to think of something," Howie said, "or Eddie's grandmother will be packing her bags and moving to Sheldon Beach. And she'll take Eddie with her."

"I can't imagine Bailey City without Eddie," Melody said softly.

"It would be terribly quiet at Bailey School," Howie admitted.

Liza's eyes got big and she grabbed

41

Eddie. "I just thought of something," she said.

"I told you to stop thinking," Eddie grumbled.

"But this is bad," Liza told him. "If you move to Sheldon Beach, you'll have to go to school with the Sheldon Sharks."

The Sheldon City School team always tried to beat Bailey School whenever they had the chance. "The Sheldon Sharks will eat me alive," Eddie moaned. "Save me!"

"It's too late," Howie said. "Jessie is ready to race."

The kids looked at the track where three motorcycles revved their engines. They lurched into action when the flag went down to start the race.

The Monster sped to the front and barreled around the track. A yellow motorcycle with orange thunderbolts gained ground as they turned the third corner. A white motorcycle with a black tornado painted on it was left behind. Around

and around the racers went. The Monster was barely able to keep ahead of the yellow motorcycle.

The yellow motorcycle was almost even with The Monster when they made their final lap. The kids saw Jessie glance over her shoulder as she neared the finish line. Just before the yellow bike was ready to take over the lead, Jessie gunned her motorcycle and sailed over the finish line in first place.

Eddie's grandmother jumped up and down and yelled at the top of her lungs.

"Jessie is one step closer to making Sheldon Beach a sea monsters' paradise," Liza said sadly.

"Not if I can help it," Howie said.

9

Poor Eddie

"My grandmother is too busy looking at pictures of resorts to even enjoy being on the beach," Eddie mumbled. "A sea monster could jump right out of the ocean and gobble me up with one big bite and she wouldn't even notice."

It was the next morning and the kids were sitting on the sand. Eddie's grandmother sat under an umbrella. A pile of magazines were scattered on the sand near her chair.

"Maybe living near the beach wouldn't be so bad," Liza told Eddie.

Melody nodded and pulled her sun visor down to block out more sun. "You could swim and build sand castles every day."

"What good would playing on the

beach be if all my friends were back in Bailey City?" Eddie asked.

"It would be very lonely," Howie admitted.

"Bailey City is the perfect place to live," Eddie said, "because that's where all my friends are."

Melody patted Eddie on the arm. "The worst part of all this," she said, "is that if Eddie moves to the beach he'll have to go to Sheldon City School. It would be impossible for him to make new friends out of the Sharks."

Eddie fell back in the sand and groaned. "I would have better luck making friends out of sand crabs," he said.

Liza pulled Eddie up from the sand. "Nothing is impossible," she told him. "Besides, maybe your grandmother will change her mind."

"My grandmother never changes her mind," Eddie complained. "She's as stubborn as a dog with a bone."

"Now we know how you learned to be so stubborn," Howie said.

"Very funny," Eddie mumbled, but he wasn't laughing. He looked like he had already lost his best friends.

"This isn't getting us anywhere," Liza said and started filling a bucket with sand. "We came to the beach for fun, so we might as well have a good time."

"What are you doing?" Melody asked.

"I'm doing what kids are supposed to

do when they're at the beach," she said. "I'm building a sand castle and you're going to help. It will take our minds off poor Eddie being devoured by the Sheldon City Sharks."

Howie nodded and worked at constructing the sand castle's tower. Liza used a paper cup to make the castle walls. Melody carved out a deep moat around the castle and used the bucket to fill it with ocean water. Eddie tried to turn a lump of sand into a moat dragon. He used a shell to carve out scales on the body. But when he started working on the dragon's snout, it all began to crumble.

Eddie threw the shell into the surf. "Nothing is turning out right," he griped.

Just then Jessie roared over the sand dune on The Monster. She headed straight for the kids. "Nice castle," she said after parking her motorcycle, "though the moat dragon could use a little work."

Liza nodded. "Eddie did a good job, but then it started to crumble."

"Maybe I can help," Jessie said. She sat down and started packing the sand. She used water from the moat to help make it hard. All four kids gathered close to watch as Jessie started molding the sand like clay. It didn't take her long to turn Eddie's dragon into a three-headed monster with a long forked tail. It looked exactly like the tattoo on her arm.

"You're good at this," Melody said politely.

Jessie smiled. "I find sea monsters very interesting," she said. "Although there is one kind I cannot stand."

"I didn't know there were different types of sea monsters," Liza said.

"There are different kinds of people, different types of cats, and different kinds of fish," Jessie pointed out as she sculpted another lump of sand into a monster with a long neck and tail. "So, of course, there would be different kinds of sea monsters.

"There is a very old story about two

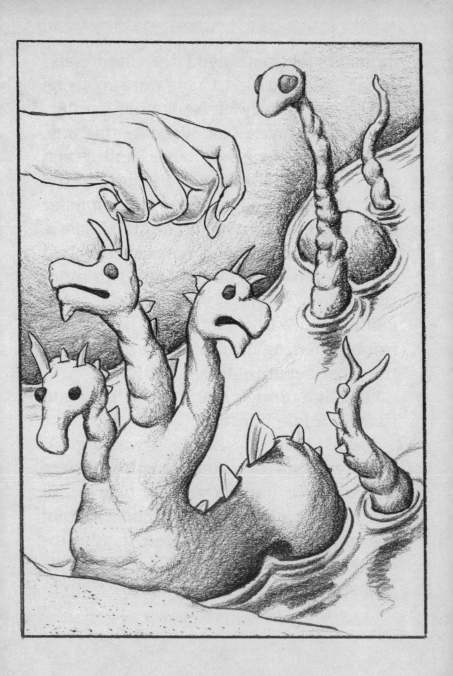

monsters that once lived deep in the sea," Jessie continued. "They were cousins and swam everywhere together, exploring hidden caves. One was like this one, with three beautiful heads and green scales that shimmered in the light of the sun. The other resembled this monster with a long skinny neck and tail." Jessie pointed to the second creature she had made before continuing. "The two monsters often found treasures hidden beneath the water, but they never had trouble sharing until one day they found the most beautiful treasure of all."

"Was it a pirate's trunk full of gold and silver?" Eddie blurted.

Jessie shook her head. "It was a giant pearl covered by rainbow colors. There was a fierce battle over the pearl until the ugly gray monster snatched it from the one who actually found it. She escaped with the pearl, and the other sea monster spent the rest of her life searching for her cousin and the stolen treasure."

"What would happen if they ever found each other?" Howie asked with a gulp.

Jessie stopped telling her story and looked at the sea monster with the long skinny neck that she had made out of sand. Then, before anyone could stop her, Jessie stood up and stomped on the sea serpent until it was nothing more than a ground-up lump of sand. "That's what would happen," Jessie said.

Then she turned and dived into the ocean.

10

Smashed

"Wow," Liza said softly. "Did you see the way Jessie smashed that sea monster?"

"It was great," Eddie said. Eddie took his fist and smashed part of the castle's wall. "Bam. It's a sea monster attack. Man the battle stations."

Melody put her hands on her hips. "Hey, watch it. You didn't make that wall. Stop tearing it up."

Liza started repairing the wall Eddie had destroyed. "You shouldn't be so mean," she said.

Eddie shrugged. "I was just having a little fun."

Howie helped Liza fix the castle. "I think we have more to worry about than sand castles," Howie told his friends.

54

Eddie fell back in the sand and made a sand angel. "You need to forget everything and relax. Try making one of these."

Howie sighed and made an angel.

"Now," Eddie said, "don't you feel better?"

"No," Howie said. "I feel worse."

"You must not be doing it right," Eddie said. "Lie down and I'll help you."

Howie laid down, but Eddie didn't help make a sand angel. Eddie started piling sand on top of Howie. The girls joined in and together they buried Howie. The only thing showing was Howie's head.

"Look," Liza said with a giggle. "Howie's a sand monster!"

"I'm stuck," Howie groaned.

Eddie's grandmother ran up to the kids and took their picture. Liza, Melody, and Eddie sat beside Howie's head. Eddie's grandmother chuckled as she went to put her camera back in her beach bag.

"Do you feel better *now*?" Eddie asked.

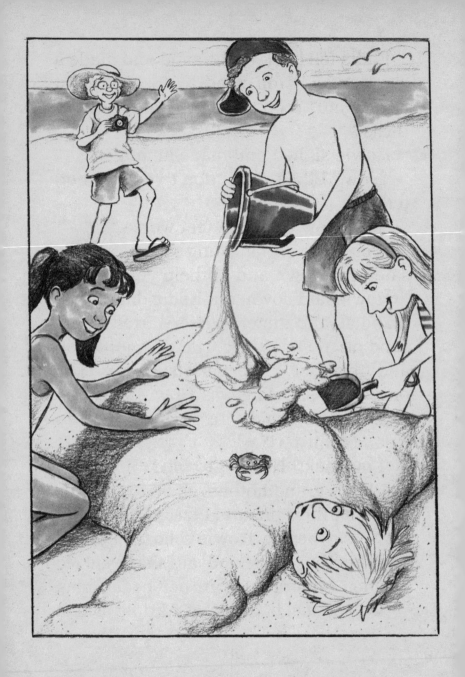

Howie groaned. "No!"

"I'm not letting you out of there until you forget about sea monsters," Eddie threatened.

Howie spat a grain of sand out of his mouth. "This is serious," he said. "Didn't you hear what Jessie said?"

"I liked her story about the sea monsters," Liza said.

"That wasn't just a story," Howie countered. "That was true. It was about Jessie and her cousin Nessie."

Melody started digging Howie out of his sand trap. "If that's true, then that means Jessie is searching for Nessie."

Howie shook sand off his body and pointed a finger at Eddie. "If Jessie finds her cousin, the entire beach resort could be smashed."

"Oh my gosh," Liza gasped. "If Eddie and his grandmother move here, they could be right in the middle of a sea monster battle."

11

No Doodle Burgers

"My grandmother can't really move," Eddie argued. "She likes it in Bailey City. She has friends and plays bridge."

"Maybe she likes it here more," Melody suggested, looking around the beach. The sand was sparkling white and the water a bright blue. Melody thought it looked like a postcard.

"We could help Eddie," Liza said. "We could tell his grandmother we don't want him to leave Bailey City."

Howie stood up and brushed sand off his legs. "Liza, you're a genius. We will talk to his grandmother. We'll show her that living at a resort isn't all fun and games."

Howie ran over to Eddie's grandmother. She was reading a thick book and a big floppy hat covered her face.

Howie grabbed a tube of sunblock and squeezed a big blob onto his hand. "We'd better put on lotion. It's dangerous to be out in the sun too long."

Eddie snatched the lotion from Howie. "I'll put some on you," Eddie told his grandmother. Eddie squirted the lotion, but it didn't go in his hand. It squirted all over his grandmother's hat and face.

"Eddie!" his grandmother shrieked. "What are you doing?"

"He's sorry," Liza said, grabbing a towel to wipe off some of the lotion. "Eddie was just trying to help. When you're at the beach you have to put on lotion all the time so you won't get sunburned."

"The sun is very bad for your skin," Melody added. "And you have to eat fish for every meal when you live at the beach."

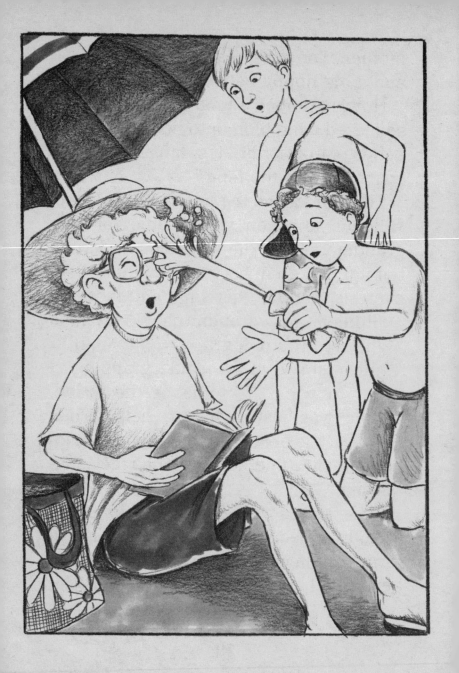

Eddie's grandmother smiled. "I don't care much for fish."

"That's all they serve in the restaurants around here," Howie said. "There's not a single Burger Doodle Restaurant in town."

Eddie's face went white. "How does anyone live without Double Onion Doodle Burgers and Doodlegum Shakes?" he asked.

"You children are exaggerating a bit." Eddie's grandmother chuckled. "I honestly think living at the beach would be wonderful."

"But what about the lotion and the fish?" Melody asked.

"And the Doodlegum Shakes?" Howie added.

"Shh," Eddie's grandmother told them. "Jessie is back from her swim. I have something to talk to her about."

The four kids groaned as Eddie's grandmother walked over to Jessie. Jessie crawled out of the surf and shook her head. Drops of water flew from her green hair. Then she stood up and smiled at Eddie's grandmother. The two grown-ups stood together while Eddie fell backward into the sand.

"My life is over," Eddie moaned.

"Poor Eddie," Liza whispered. "I'm so worried about him."

Howie nodded toward Jessie. "I think we need to worry about the sea monster."

The kids gulped as Jessie dug into the pocket of her leather suit and handed Eddie's grandmother an envelope.

12

Good-bye, Bailey City

"I have a surprise for you," Eddie's grandmother sang the next morning during breakfast.

Eddie rubbed his eyes and yawned. "It's too early for surprises," he groaned.

Eddie's grandmother didn't pay any attention to Eddie. She reached in her pocket and pulled out five pieces of paper. "Jessie was kind enough to give us free tickets for the races today," she told Melody, Howie, Liza, and Eddie.

Howie swallowed his juice with one big gulp. "Jessie races today?" Howie asked.

Eddie's grandmother smiled. "Today is the big championship race," she explained with a wink. "I can't wait for you to see it!"

The kids piled into Eddie's grand-mother's van after breakfast. Nobody said a word as they pulled into the parking lot at the raceway. Eddie's grand-mother was in such a hurry she beat Eddie to the ticket booth. They had barely found their seats in the bleachers when Eddie's grandmother jumped up. "I . . . um . . . need to find Jessie," she stammered. "We have some special plans to discuss. You'll be okay for a little while, won't you?"

Howie nodded. "We'll wait for you right here," he told Eddie's grandmother before she hopped down the stairs and disappeared in the stands.

Eddie groaned and slid down in his seat. "She's looking for Jessie," he said. "That means she must have made up her mind to move to Sheldon Beach."

Eddie slumped down in his seat. He didn't even see the motorcycles getting ready for the big race. "My life is over,"

Eddie moaned. "I might as well say good-bye to Bailey City forever!"

Melody patted Eddie on the back. Liza sniffed. Howie had to blink back tears. "Life won't be the same without Eddie," Howie said.

They were all so busy feeling sorry for themselves, they hardly noticed when the flag was dropped to start the big race.

Jessie's slime-green motorcycle lurched to the front of the pack, and the race was

on. One rider skidded off the track at the second corner, but a yellow motorcycle zipped around him and started gaining on Jessie.

"It looks like Jessie has this race in the bag," Eddie groaned. "If she wins another race she could have enough money to buy the resort where I'll have to move."

"Wait!" Lisa squealed. "There's a new bike in the race, and it's gaining on Jessie."

Eddie sat up to watch as a bright red

motorcycle with purple lightning bolts passed four other riders to challenge Jessie. The kids watched the motorcycles go around and around the track.

The motorcycles roared around the track. The Monster was in the lead, but the bright red bike gained ground. They were tied as they raced toward the finish line. Suddenly, the red motorcycle revved its engine and lurched ahead of Jessie's bike to cross the finish line first.

The crowd jumped up and roared. Howie, Liza, and Melody clapped and screamed. Eddie hopped on his seat and did a dance.

The reporter from WMTJ rushed to interview the new winner.

"I wonder who beat Jessie!" Howie yelled above the crowd's noise.

"Whoever it is," Eddie hollered, "he's a hero to me because maybe now I won't have to move!"

Just then, the new racer pulled off his

helmet to talk with the reporter from WMTJ.

The entire crowd grew silent.

"What's wrong?" Melody asked as the four kids looked down at the track.

That's when Eddie saw the new winner. "It can't be!" he cried.

13

Sea Monster Hunt

The winning rider was another woman. But she wasn't just any woman. She was Eddie's grandmother!

The kids rushed down from the stands. Eddie's grandmother brushed back her gray curls and laughed when the reporter from WMTJ asked why she wanted to start racing at her age.

"Age doesn't mean a thing. I'm always looking for new adventures," she said, "and now I've found one. Racing motorcycles!"

"Where's Jessie?" Melody whispered.

Howie glanced at the crowd. "There she is," he said and pointed. Jessie stood off to the side, looking at a map.

Howie, Liza, and Melody left Eddie with his grandmother. They weaved

71

through the crowd until they were at Jessie's side. "I hope you're not too disappointed about losing," Liza said politely.

When Jessie shook her head her green hair swayed, reminding Howie of ocean waves. "Losing is part of competing," she explained. "Besides, I have decided not to stay at Sheldon Beach to race."

"But what will you do if you don't race your motorcycle?" Melody asked.

Jessie looked toward the ocean. "I plan to hunt for my cousin," she said. "I have an idea where she may have gone."

Jessie folded up her map and climbed on The Monster. "Besides," she told the kids with a smile, "you never know when I might be back!"

Jessie started The Monster. She waved as she roared away.

"I guess we're finally safe from sea monsters," Liza said.

Howie watched Jessie until The Monster turned a corner and disappeared

from sight. "I hope her sea monster hunt doesn't lead her right to Bailey City," he said with a frown. But Melody and Liza had already turned to join Eddie and his grandmother. Howie hurried to catch up.

Eddie sat on his grandmother's shining motorcycle. His grandmother laughed when he made roaring sounds.

"Are you still thinking about moving to the beach?" Howie asked Eddie's grandmother.

She shook her head and smiled. "You kids were right," she told all four friends. "Sitting on the beach day after day is not my idea of an adventure. Jessie convinced me that riding motorcycles is much more fun!"

Eddie slapped his forehead and grinned. "I can't believe it," he said. "Grandmothers don't ride motorcycles—or do they?"